overview

So i am jayden gotham the owner and founder of gotham entertainment and i was set the task of writing a story for a competition so here is a overview Literature Works is teaming up with Plymouth City Council, Plymouth Culture and the With Flying Colours project, reaching out to aspiring young writers in the city between the ages of 14 and 19 years, as we seek the next Plymouth Young City Laureate.

The role of Plymouth Young City Laureate is important. The chosen young writer will be commissioned to create work to celebrate special events or occasions in the city and will be invited to perform in libraries schools and at festivals.

We will commission the successful 2022-23 Young City Laureate on three occasions and pay a fee of £50 per commission. We will ask the Young City Laureate to perform at least two events across the year, alongside invited writers, for which they will also be paid.

Who can apply?

The Young City Laureate is open to **any young person aged 14-19** who lives, works or studies in Plymouth. You will be a writer of either **prose** (fiction, creative non-fiction) or **poetry**.

How to apply

If you are interested in this role, please submit:

1. **A 200-word statement** about why you would like to be the Young City Laureate for Plymouth and what you would do with the role if you got it. (You might want to tell us about people or organisations you'd like to work with or events you'd like to be part of, for example).

2. **Two pieces of creative writing**. These should be either poetry (no more than one page of A4 per poem), or prose in the form of fiction or creative non-fiction (no more than 2,000 words per piece). Your writing should address these topics:

❖ **'Plymouth: A Welcoming City'** – why is Plymouth welcoming? What makes it feel like home?

❖ **#WritingCommunity** – what is it like to be a young writer? #WritingCommunity is a popular hashtag used by writers on social media to share their day to day experience of writing. As your response, please tell the reader what it's like for you to be writing today in Plymouth.

So here is game zones the campfire of Plymouth

Chapter 1

A 200-word statement

Oh hi there, my name is Jayden Gotham. I have made a script and shown it to a director at Theatre Royal Plymouth and they have redirected me here and I love an adventure even if it is a book, a performance or an event. I love to entertain but I do things differently. Right now I am an actor for Gotham Entertainment, a year of fun.
I love to make people think and leave them wondering about the world around us… Everything I do always ends with something that will blow your mind, leaving you thirsty for more. If I successfully became Plymouth's next Young Laureate, I would use my entertaining personality to support key family events in and around Plymouth.

In everything I do I always follow a thing I made up called the beacons of entertainment they are fun, immersive, wonder, together and entertainment and I always strive to do things that have neither been done before like paper boy and bookical (a book-musical) I would do anything to entertain people I hope the one reader is still here reading because there is one thing you need to know.
To be continued.
In the campfire of Plymouth

Chapter 2

‘Plymouth: A Welcoming City’ 2000-word story

“Because there is one thing you need to know is to be continued,” said Jayden in a scary voice

“that is not scary” shouted Joe.

“I know what is scary,” Said Jayden “are you ready”

“Yes of course,” said Joe

“we'll see about that,” said Jayden

“A hundred years ago in a city, we call Plymouth, was home to the ogre’s war a deadly war between good and bad magic the one that wiped our minds and trapped us in a simulation”.

“Aaaaa scary,” said Joe sarcastically

“Just you wait,” said Jayden

“People died and only some lived, the ghost of the ones who haunt the streets of Plymouth and the one next to you looking over your head as you are reading this”

“No stop!” shouted Joe

“Every night the wall between the spirit world and ours is getting thinner but they are no longer good they are more than evil and there is only one person that can stop it
and his name is Joe”.

“What me,” said Joe

“Yes you,” said Jayden

Jayden and Joe are sitting around a campfire and all of a sudden purple smoke starts to fly around Jayden with wind flowing around and an older man appears with glowing blue eyes and magic coming out of his hands.

“Listen Joe” the old man exclaimed “our world needs your help so follow me”

Suddenly Joe and the man disappear then reappear in a big big big big room

“Joe here is the wall of legends the people who stopped the war and here is the master bumbum”

“Hahahaha I'm sorry” chuckled Joe

“He is the leader of the legends! but back to the task Plymouth is in danger, the ghost off whom have died will soon come out and possess everyone and only you can stop them, you need to get the orb and trap them.”

“And where can I get that from,” said Joe

“From the top of mound humongous the universes deadly volcano
But before you go take this scroll and record everything”

“Wait,” said Joe
“Off you go,” said the man
“No no,” said Joe
“Bye,” said the man

And just like Donald trump, puff and he is gone to the bottom of mound humongous

Intro (challenge (for you) read this in a deep voice)

A hundred years ago the legends wrote upon a scroll to stop a deadly war that no one knows until the night will arrive and the ghost of the ones that died will possess the ones that live.
But only one can stop this, this adventure that they have been given and this is one you will not want to miss (or is it(i am just reading the script))

Chapter 3 death hill

“Ok,” said Joe
“And what do I do I have nothing to do I am total not lost in a land I don't know and total not about to lose it”

Ten seconds later
“Ahhhhhhhhhhhhhhhhhhhhhhhhhhhhhhhh” he screams with an echo
“Come on Joe you need to save Plymouth I need to get up the volcano”

“Oh hello there,” said a strange girl’s voice

“Who are you,” said Joe scared

“I am Debra but call me Deb for short,” she said coming out from the dark
“And why are you here” questioned, Joe
“I ask that sometimes,” said, Deb
“Anyway I need to get up there,” said, Joe
“Wait no going up there is an act of suicide,” said, Deb
“Can you please help me?” said Joe
“No,” said Deb
“Please”
“No”
“Why”
“No”
Argues Joe and Deb
“Guess what,” said Joe
“No” replied Deb
“We are halfway up the mount,” said Joe
“Noooooooooooooooooooo” shouted Deb “ok I will help you but just this once why do you want to get up there”

“To save Plymouth,” said Joe

“And why do you want to save that place,” said Deb

“I don't know, it is my home the feel of people welcoming you there are some bad people but most of them are good, they all love a conversion and i do have to give back because I have done some bad stuff,” said Joe

“What said” Deb

“Nosy,” said Joe

“Wait what did you say is going to happen in Plymouth” questioned Deb

“Plymouth and ghost will come from the dead,” said Joe

“No he is back,” said Deb

“What,” said Joe

“The ogre’s war happened one hundred years ago right and it is suddenly the ghost are coming out now and it is all happening now it can't be a guidance something is doing it or someone with the name of wes,” said Deb

“How do you know him,” said Joe

“Wes was my friend he is also known as Mr Goatman well loved in this land and he lived across a river but one day he was walking across the Goatman bridge when a cult that I am forbidden to name ambushed him got a rope and tied one end to the bridge and the other to his neck and push him off and the cult left,the next day they went back and found that he was not there and decided to burn down his house killing the rest of his family Wes turned evil and uses ghost to get revenge, you need to go now we need to get up that mount,” said Deb

“Let's go,” they said

Day one dear scroll
Me and my new friend are running up mount Humongous in a race against time to save Plymouth from Wes……………….

Deb and Joe were running up the mountain as fast as they can to get the orb and they have got it

“Now go and save Plymouth,” said Deb

“Will i see you again?” said Joe

“I don't know but go and save Plymouth,” said Deb

“Thank you,” said Joe

“Bye and remember you are the writer and you are the key,” said Deb

End of chapter 3

Chapter 4 evil is the problem

Present day location unknown
“Ha my plan is working,” said Wes “just a couple more things then Plymouth will end Vaze come here”

“hi master,” said Vaze as he jumps out

“Ahhhh don’t do that there is just one more thing I need and that is that scroll” shouted Wes

Present day location city centre

“Aaaaaand I am stuck again,” said Joe

“Joe” shouted a mysterious voice

“Bill” shouted Joe “is that you”

“Where have you been,” said Bill

“I don't even know these days,” said Joe “actually let me explain”

1 day later

“O….k….” said Bill

“So can you help me,” said Joe

“Yes I can, what did Deb say before you left,” said Bill

“She said something like *you are the writer and you are the key,”* said Joe

“Yeah what do writers do,” said Bill

“They write stories,” said Joe

“And where do the stories go,” said Bill

“The library said” Bill and Joe

“Coming,” said Joe

“Yes,” said Bill

Present day location unknown

“Hurry up,” said Wes “oh, I have an incoming call, hello this is Wes from your death is the best speaking, how can i help”

“I know who you are and you know who I am,” said unknown

“DEB” shouted Wes “what do you want”

“I want you to stop,” said Deb

“Well you want me to stop,” said Wes “you are so dumb i am not that stupid”

“Well you do look it,” said Deb “we used to be friends”

“Oh where’s my violin,” said Wes

“Oh hello,” said the man

“Oh i hate zoom,” said Wes

“Zoom?” Said Deb and the man

“I do prefer the sky,” said the man

“Sky broadband?” Said Wes

“No magic,” said, Deb

“Oh like a magic wand,” said Wes

“Harry Potter,” said the man

“JUST END THE CALL,” said Wes, Deb and the man

(end of call)

Present day location library

“Oh what is this” said Joe

“You are too young to look at that,” said Bill pushing Joe away from that book “and now I am stuck”

“We need to look at a row of books and I know with the clue that Deb has given us, you are the writer. When I was writing a book once I dropped my jam sandwich and it splattered all over the floor and I got my cat to clean it up. What happened next? Oh then my plate spilled on my laptop, I opened the lid to see if it was working the time was 9:90 …. It is on row 990 “said Joe

“Ok?” Question Bill

“Let's go,” said Joe and Bill

Joe and Bill looked all through the night until they found the book and the book was called Drakes island

“So I need to go to Drakes island,” said Joe

“Yes,” said Bill “I will stay here you go”

“Ok bye” shouted Joe

Joe left the library and started to go but all of a sudden

“Ha got you,” said Vaze

<u>End of chapter 4</u>

<u>Chapter 5 evil is the end</u>

Present day location ~~unknown~~ **Drakes island**

"Wes why are you doing this," said Joe panicking

“Because I am and for my plan to work I need the heart from the most created soul and that is what you are for,” said Wes

“Listen i know you have been through a lot but hurting people is not the way please listen,” said Joe

“Oh maybe…. Not kill him” said Wes

“Not you don’t,” said Deb and Bill

“Haha you idiots you know by having the person with a magical soul in the room now i can start it in 3,2,1 go,” said Wes

“We need to go,” said Bill

“Listen you the only way to stop this is if you write your ending go quick,” said Deb

“Ok,” said Joe

Day two dear scroll

I am racing against time to save Plymouth and writing the ending writing as fast as I can I struggled going through lots of drafts until I have got it

“Have you done it?” said, Deb

“Yes,” said Joe

“Now are you ready,” said Deb

“Will I see you again?” said Joe

“I don't know”, said Deb, “but we need to do this ready …. 3”

“2,” said Bill

“1,” said Joe

All of a sudden the ghost disappears along with Deb and Wes gets sucked into the book with Joe going back to the hall of legends

“Well done Joe,” said the man

“Where am I, oh I am here,” said Joe

“Rude but anyway you have saved the wonderful city of Plymouth you have trapped Wes and the ghost in the book and that book with being locked up here but you need to go back to the campfire and have a rest but i need to wipe you mind of the adventure you have just been on,” said the man

“But no” shouted joe “I want to remember this adventure”

“You can't be able to remember your mind can open the book without you knowing Bill and Deb had their minds wiped already and after this mine will join them,” said the man

“Ok if I have to,” said Joe.

“But there is one thing you will remember that you are on the wall of legends,” said the man “Now hold this crystal and think of the warm campfire and the city of Plymouth”

“Plymouth, fire” chanted Joe.

And on the 3rd time, Joe disappears and goes back to the camp.

“Well what an adventure you have just witnessed reading this yes I am a man but I still struggle but I just kept on going and just put my mind to it, like what Joe and his new friends did and that is what you should do and may be wondering what my name is and I can tell you but you will have to find out but there is one thing that I can tell you is”… ***said Jayden***

To be continued

Chapter 6

#WritingCommunity 1-page poem

After my adventure
Have released 20 books
And a lot more to come
That trip on magic has made me a new friend
(that is a good title for joe and his friend)
And that is why I am on the way
For the release of my new book
The campfire of Plymouth
Away to share my adventure with my kids
And you can do that yourself
Pick up a pen and write your mind
And share it with the world
You neither know you could be sitting around the campfire
But before I go
on my adventure
I have found out
that is the reason why the present day is called that
Is because it is a present
a gift is given to you
and when you open it,
it is a surprise and if you tell someone what is in the present in the past
it will ruin the future
and you probably thought this will be 11 pages of foul language
, **** off,
but the older I get the more I realise the world is getting disposable,
disposable nappies,
disposable phone,
even disposable banks and governments
and you start to think there is nothing you can rely on
but pop to the library and get yourself a book
if it is Roald Dahl to David Walliams
there will always be a friend
and a book is what you can rely on
did you know that your friends are not your only friend
the people who are not your friend are your other friend
they are just too scared to admit it
because your mate is your mate until they take a wife,
a book is your friend all your life
but just remember you can always count on the writers of the magic
the people that put the k in a book
the #writingcommunity
because you can rely on us
we will always be there for you
even when you don't realise.

The end

By Jayden Gotham
Made for you

For any complaints please send them to the mailing address,
1 Apple Park Way
I love your feedback and complaints because the more complaints we have the bigger the bonfire and more chance of there being a sequel of 'the campfire of Plymouth

Thank you
Jayden gotham
The owner and founder of Gotham Entertainment
J.G

WELCOME TO GOTHAM ENTERTAINMENT

Gotham Entertainment

FUN I IMMERSIVE I ENTERTAINMENT

Gotham entertainment is an interactive business to immerse you into our story line and witness real magic right before you eyes. Our amazing castmembers bring you all the comedy, drama and action to you. We also have The Magic Theatre which brings a broadway style performance to your party. We have Dj Jay who brings the magic of music to your party but if you cant order us you can still get the taste of magic with our immersive franchise which links in with Den production, Game zone, The Magic Theatre company or even lazer. With all of this and our iconic characters with the Gotham gang and their adventures. We have puppet paradise with there silliness or even the cast of gotham entertainment with their drama. when we make entertainment we follow by the beacons of entertainment which are fun, immersive, wonder, together and entertainment. so no matter where you are we will bring fun entertainment because we are Gotham entertainment and we are fun ,immersive, entertainment

find us at

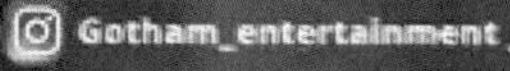

fun for all ages

a magical experience

To find more books and stuff like this check out the game zone amazon page

Den productions and game zones the campfire of Plymouth the movie Coming to 2024

Comming soon